DEDICATION

I would like to thank Suzanne and Barbara for all their encouragement to put my book together and my partner Wizz for his support and title for the book.

CONTENTS

THE WRITER'S GROUP

Late again, as usual! *Why am I always late for everything*? She thought. One day I will be on time, she promised herself. That is, if there is a group to come to in the future. Not if one person had their way that was for sure.

It all started about three months ago, she was chatting to Nicky on the phone, the day after one of their monthly writer's group meetings. Nicky wasn't feeling too well and she had taken the day off work with stomach problems. She could completely sympathise, she wasn't feeling too good herself.

'Maybe there's a bug going around.' She said to Nicky.

The following month, the day after the meeting; feeling uneasy and again not too well, she phoned Nicky.

'I'm really not feeling great, how are you?'

'Not good,' said Nicky 'this is strange, feeling ill again the day after the group meeting. Do you think it's something in Pam's house?'

That was where they met for the writing group.

'What do you mean?' She asked. 'Like Legionaries or something?'

'Oh ignore me,' replied Nicky, 'it's a crazy idea. Maybe we are being poisoned by Pam's baking.' And with that she laughed.

'Don't tell her that!' She exclaimed, with a giggle. 'And anyway, I didn't have any of her cakes last night, I'm on yet another diet, but I still feel awful.'

So with some trepidation she was going to the meeting a month later. Pam welcomed her at the front door and ushered her into the dining room, which the group occupied for their meetings.

'Hi everyone,' she said looking around the dining room table. 'sorry I'm late.'

'So what's new!' Said Rick jokingly.

Nicky was sat down next to Rick, then the other members of the group; Carol, Jane, Owen, Alice, but no George! He was never late, always very diligent and gentlemanly, although he could be a bit cutting with his criticism of the other members writing submissions.

'Right everyone,' said Pam. 'I was unsure about holding the meeting this evening. I got a phone call, only about half an hour ago from George's wife Esther, poor George passed away about three weeks ago. He had a bad bout of gastroenteritis and unfortunately because of his heart condition there was nothing the doctors could do.'

'Oh poor George.' Exclaimed Nicky, with tears welling up in her eyes.

'From what I've been hearing, I think we've all had a bout of that.' Said Alice

'Not me,' replied Owen. 'I've a stomach like cast iron.'

'Anyway whatever it was,' said Pam 'at least we have recovered unlike poor George.'

'Shall we all just have tea and cake tonight?' suggested Jane 'And share our memories of George.'

'That's a very good idea.' With that, Pam went into the kitchen to put the kettle on.

'Let me help.' Said Nicky

She looked around the group enquiringly. 'Everyone for tea as usual, except you Owen, have you got your own tipple?' Nicky asked him with a slight frown on her face.

'Yes I have love, thanks.' He replied.

Owen was a bit OCD about eating and drinking when in other people's houses, so he always brought his own bottle of flavoured water, which he drank straight from the bottle, always refusing a glass for it.

I wonder, she thought as she watched Nicky follow Pam into the kitchen, was Owen a poisoner? No, that's positively ridiculous, and anyway he never leaves his chair until he's ready to go. It couldn't be Pam, she loved this group and positively thrived on it. She nurtured each one of them, wanting them all to become successful writers. She looked round the table at the others just as Pam entered the room with her cake stand ladled with delicious home baked cakes.

'Oh my god!' She cried out, as she got up from the table and darted into the kitchen.

'Nicky what are you doing?'

Nicky turned around startled, knocking a cup of tea from the worktop together with a small packet. She immediately burst into tears.

'It's not my fault, I just wanted to teach you all a lesson. You were all so horrible about me.'

'What do you mean?'

'I heard you all a few months ago, after the meeting; remember when I came back because I had left my keys in the hall. None of you realised I had been stood for a few minutes listening to all of you. How you felt sorry for me and I would never be a writer in a million years.'

She did remember, it was true, they had been trying to think of a way to gently let Nicky know. The whole group had now congregated in the kitchen, to see what was going on.

'So you have been poisoning us.' said Carol incredulously.

'Yes' said Nicky defiantly. 'You all deserved it.'

'But you were ill as well Nicky, when I phoned you.'

'I was pretending, I had hoped to get away with this.'

'What about me?' asked Owen. 'You couldn't poison me!'

No I couldn't, you have been a thorn in my side how to deal with you. I was going to have to take a couple of years in prison for you, when I *accidentally,'* she gestured with fingers curled in the air, 'ran you over.'

Nicky did serve time in prison for the attempted murder of six people and the suspected manslaughter of poor old George. Manslaughter because despite her confession, the poison she used is colourless and odourless and non-specific in post mortem, as a cause of death.

Nicky did however, during her time in prison write and self publish a novel based on a writing group. It turned out to be a best-seller and she donated all the money to the British Heart Foundation. Not I hasten to say, out of any remorse but to prove to the others she was better than them, as she always knew she was!

DOUBLE TAKE

Rose stood in the hallway, staring at her reflection in the mirror. Looking deeply into her own blue eyes, so many questions she may never have the answer to. Does she have blue eyes like me? She thought, or maybe they are brown like my sister's. Desperately trying to imagine her own face some twenty years older. What if she bumped into her in the street, would she even know her?

If only, thought Rose, but life wouldn't be that kind. There was no way her mother would recognise her. She had only been eighteen months old and her sister just turned three years old, when they had been abandoned by her. Left in a derelict factory. Had she meant them to die before they would be discovered? This was the question that had tormented her, all her young life.

Marjorie her sister refused to talk about it. Their paternal aunt Agnes had grudgingly brought them up. Only because she wanted to be seen as a martyr in the neighbourhood. A good pious woman! Pious, okay, Rose would concede that without doubt, but good? That was a joke. In Rose's estimation the woman was a monster. That woman never wasted a moment in telling the two sisters what a slut their mother was a waster and a user.

After their father had been killed in action in the D Day landings, their mother apparently, according to Agnes; had taken to going out nightly to the local dance hall, leaving the two young sisters on their own. Flirting and giving her body to any man who would by her a drink, or a yank who could supply her with stockings.

Rose reflected about the comparison between Agnes and what she knew of her mother. At least her mother had shown signs of passion and needs. Unlike her sister in law who was a shrivelled old spinster, who tutted and scoffed at any demonstration of affection. The woman had tried to force her views and attitudes on the young sisters, and to some extent she had been successful with Marjorie. She had turned on Rose a few times and made comments like, *I bet you are going to turn out just like our mother.* This was obviously meant to hurt Rose and if their aunt overheard, Rose knew there would be a smug self satisfied look on her face.

Rose had learned to build up a hard, protective shield around her feelings, never giving anything away. When Marjorie had run out of the school playground crying, after suffering the taunts of the other kids; *your mother didn't want you, she wanted you to die.* Rose would always stand her ground defiantly, saying nothing, staring at the young tormentors. Refusing to give way to the tears that she thought she would surely drown in, if she ever let them escape. Yes she thought, life had been tough but at least now she could see a way out. She was fourteen now and had a job at the factory. She planned to save every penny she could, apart from what her aunt took from her for her keep, then she would move away and leave the hateful woman and hopefully never set eyes on her again!

She let out an inaudible sigh and was jolted from her thoughts by her aunt's voice behind her.

'You still here, stop your idle daydreaming and get to the shops with that list. You will be the death of me girl.' If only, thought Rose. Maybe there is a God in heaven.

Leaving the small terraced house she set off down the road to the high street, stuffing the shopping list in her coat pocket. Carrying her aunt's clumsy wicker basket that scratched her bare legs when it was full. *Oh stuff this,* she thought and with that she threw the basket over the iron railings into the school playground. *I'm going into town to the new Woolworths store.* She had been a few weeks ago and had wandered around thinking it was like an Aladdin's cave; a shop full of so many different things. She might even ask if there were any jobs going. Something that would be much better than the dreary old factory where her aunt was good friends with the female supervisor.

Casting aside the thought of what her aunt would say when she got back, she practically jumped on the double decker bus that would take her into town. Feeling nervous but rebellious, she arrived in the town centre. Getting off the bus she was almost skipping up the main road heading towards the store. In her hurry she nearly bumped into the woman coming out.

'Be careful love.' said the woman.

Rose did a double take, looking directly into the woman's face. So unmistakably like her own but older.

'Mum?' she said as she collapsed and fell to the ground.

NATURE'S WICKED TRICKS

I used to smell of Chanel No 5, most days now it's Voltarol. I used to have a spring in my step, now I've got titanium screws in my hips. At one time, a pain in the neck was someone I found annoying, now I'm off to the physio with the pain in my neck. It goes without saying, surely the face in the mirror belongs to someone much older than me! The hearing is going - sometimes a blessing. The lens in the glasses are getting stronger, or is there a conspiracy to make print smaller? But I'm still standing!

THE VISITATION

'So are you all ready to go?'

'I think so.' Replied Roger.

A slight hesitation in his voice. He looked around the room fondly. This has been his home for the last five years. He had been happy here, more than he ever expected to be. But all things come to an end and it was time for him to move on. There were some things he wished he could take with him, then again they are only things, he thought.

'Give me your hand Roger and your soul.' Said the angel. 'You will have a safe passage.'

THE LONGING

She lies in bed, her half of the king size but she's almost on the edge. She feels uncomfortable and stiff on her right side. She has been lying in this position all night, sleeping fitfully as she does every night now. Not wanting to be close or even have to face her husband of many years; abhorrent even to the thought of his breath on her face.

She must have dozed off again, because now is the sound of the alarm clock going off. Oh how she loathes that sound, she pulls her hand out from under the duvet and switches it off. The cold air in the room immediately envelopes the bare skin of her arm, but she leaves it there outstretched, she no longer cares about such sensations. Opening her eyes, it's dark although it's 7am but it is winter.

As she lies there and is aware of the steady breathing of her husband, her heart sinks with the realization she has woken up. So yet again her prayers of the previous night, as all the prayers of so many nights before, have not been answered. She drags herself wearily out of bed reaching for her dressing gown from the chair next to her side of the bed. She wonders whether she really possesses the will and energy to get through the day.

Leaving her sleeping husband, he will stay there until she shakes him awake so that he has time to get ready for work, she makes her way downstairs into the kitchen. The blinds are open at the window, she stands there looking out onto the garden while waiting for the kettle to boil. There is just the first glimmer of sunrise, it's going to be a beautiful day, she has to acknowledge that at least. With a clear sky and a heavy frost that has formed overnight, there is a sparkly magical touch to the appearance to the garden. In times past she would have loved getting up to a morning like this. Not now! How can it all look so normal? Everything looks so familiar as she looks around the clean and very tidy kitchen, but it's almost as if she's an onlooker, not part of it anymore, disassociated, cast adrift in what once was her life.

The kettle boils and she pours the water into her cup with the teabag in. Sitting down at the small kitchen table she sips the tea slowly. Strange how it doesn't really taste of anything, but it has to be done because it's part of the morning timetable. Rinsing her cup and putting it in the dishwasher, she glances up at the clock on the wall, seven thirty. It's time to wake him up.

Walking slowly back up the stairs, her thoughts too intrusive, how does she get through another day? As she enters the bedroom, apart from the sound of her still sleeping husband, there is a lullaby playing softly in the room.

Standing motionless, confused looking around the still dark room she can make out the familiar shapes of the furniture. Her eyes come to rest on the small sofa where she has placed her daughter's collection of teddy bears; including the small brown bear that plays a lullaby when the key is turned in the middle of it's back.

It has been many years since she wound the little bear and placed him in her daughter's cot a bedtime.

As the tears fall silently down her face, she whispers her daughter's name. A small glimmer of hope rises in her conscious mind.

Today, she can go on and maybe all the days after. To her this is a sign that in some way her child is still with her.

PERFECT LIAISON

‘We’re quite busy this evening.’ She said.

‘We certainly are.’ He replied.

‘Think you have been in more demand than me, but that is to be expected, don’t you agree?’ She asked without any feelings of animosity or jealousy.

‘Yes it’s the way things are now, as long as they don’t separate us, I’m happy, are you?’

‘I’m always happy when I’m with you, we are just perfect together.’

‘Oh here we go, customers, am I looking my best dear?’ He asked

‘You always do darling.’ She looked him up and down affectionately.

‘Well it’s important we don’t let our standards drop.’

They are sitting at our table darling. Look like a nice couple don’t they? Hopefully they will have nice table manners, you can’t always tell straight away.’

‘No indeed! Are you thinking about the family who came in a couple of days ago?’

‘Yes,’ she said. ‘Those children were just unbearable, eating with their fingers and using the tablecloth to wipe their grubby hands on.’

‘I can’t understand why the manager let them in.’ He retorted. ‘Just because people have money doesn’t mean they know how to behave.’

‘No unfortunately not.’ She said in agreement. ‘Luckily we don’t get too many like them.’

‘Oh look out, I think he’s going to ask her to marry him.’

‘What makes you think that?’ She asks quizzically.

‘He has that nervous look, half terrified she will reject him, but playing with the cutlery and napkin in an excited way. He can’t keep his hands still, hoping she is going to say yes.’

‘You old romantic, I know it makes you happy to see those in love leave after their meal, hand in hand planning their future together.’

‘I know,’ he sighed, ‘but it is far better than when it all goes wrong; the rejection, the tears, the banging down on the table, shaking us to our very core. I really don’t like that.’

‘They can’t all be as happy as us, we were made for each other.’

‘We absolutely were.’ He responded, swelling with pride. ‘I won’t argue with that. So what do you think darling, are we going to be a double act tonight?’

‘I think you may be flying solo tonight as usual, but you know I don’t mind.’ She says lovingly. ‘This young couple look far too health conscious to want me on their food.’

‘Here I go.’ He says.

The young man at their table lifts the pepper grinder to his food, while the salt grinder looks on with love and admiration.

AUSTERITY

'I'm really not comfortable with this, they have spent a lifetime together!' She looked at the other two imploringly.

'I can't see what other option there is, we don't have the funds to keep them together.' He explained. 'After all the husband is still reasonably well and does not need the care the wife does.'

'But this couple, already in their nineties, should end their days together in the companionship of each other. Surely this is the humane thing to do?'

'I've just received an email,' said the note taker, 'problem solved, the husband has taken his own life.'

THE PLAN

She will make it happen, it's her lifelong dream to walk down the aisle and marry the man she loves. He thought she was joking when she first mentioned it, and she had laughed to cover her embarrassment, but then she had walked out of the room, to contain her anger. Everything was done; the venue booked, the dress bought, the flowers chosen, the guests invited and all sworn to secrecy. It was going to be the perfect day! Then he had to go and ruin it. His suit just doesn't look right, with that knife in his chest.

CONCEALMENT

Josie tapped on the door politely as she had been trained to do, just in case the guest had not vacated the room. Some of them not able or inclined to leave by the checkout time of 11am, She listened carefully, her ear pressed against the door.

'Housekeeping.'

No sounds coming from within but with this particular guest, that didn't particularly mean anything. The woman had been booked in to stay over the weekend. After checking in, she had gone to her room and it seems she had not left it all weekend. Not even making an appearance at breakfast or evening meals! The 'do not disturb' on her door had been honoured, so apart from Heather on reception who had booked her in, none of the other staff had any contact with the guest.

Satisfied the room was empty she opened the door with the master key. The room was very tidy almost as if no one had stayed there, except the tea and coffee making facilities had been used. The bed linen had been straightened so it look neat. This was going to be an easy clean she thought, as she walked into the bathroom, which again showed little sign of use. But then as she looked around she saw what looked like a faint smear of blood on the side of the wash basin. Oh well, Josie thought, I will have to do some cleaning then! She didn't really want this job, but as an impoverished student at the local university and with no wealthy parents to support her through her degree, there wasn't any choice.

After a cursory but adequate clean of the bathroom, she made a start on the bedroom and, as was her habit, she checked the drawers and wardrobes in case the guests ever left anything of value, that may not be claimed. It was a risk, admittedly, but she figured if you could afford to stay at this up-market hotel, the odd trinket or mislaid cash would make little or no difference and the guests could always claim on their insurance.

There was nothing to be found in the drawers. She went to check the wardrobe next and there it was. She couldn't quite believe what she was seeing! Grotesque yet somehow strangely beautiful at the same time, a tiny newborn life cut short for whatever reason. The tiny infant's body wrapped in a towel and laid on a pillow.

Josie didn't scream, she was a tough cookie, the product of a difficult childhood. Reaching out to touch the infants face, she knew already by the pallor of it's skin it was dead. Mesmerised her finger gently stroked it's crinkled little face and unusual for her, the tears rolled silently down her cheeks.

Thousand of miles away at Dubai airport arrivals lounge, walks an impeccably dressed woman in her Armani suit and flawlessly applied makeup. The latter hopefully to conceal the paleness of her complexion and swollen eyelids, the result of the nightmarish weekend! Which she hoped with all her heart, that neither the husband who she hadn't seen in many months; coming forward to greet her, or the lover she has left behind forever. Will ever find out.

JUSTICE WILL BE MINE

He has no idea I am sitting so close to him, so close I can almost feel his breath on my face. I have waited months for this opportunity, he doesn't know me at all but I'm positive he will he recognise my voice, if I get the chance to speak. Probably not though, he speaks to dozens of people about different topics every week.

He knows nothing about me. If he did he may have treated me with more respect. I know so much about him, not only where he lives, what car he drives; the coffee shops he frequents with his colleagues, and of course restaurants where he dines with that pretty wife of his. I might stand a chance with her. I'm a good looking guy and she is to become a vulnerable grieving widow. Anyway, I'm jumping ahead of myself here. There is a lot to be done first, and despite the warm stirrings in my groin when I think of her, I keep my expression relaxed and neutral as I look at his despicable face.

Just like any other member of the studio audience, I listen to the current topic being debated waiting for my chance to contribute. Of course this is all banal mutterings to me, sat with these stupid people who believe what they say and think actually matters. I proved months ago when I phoned into this programme, that my thought processes and beliefs are far superior to anything they could conjure up in their small minds.

I'm waiting though, putting my hand up for the microphone to come my way. I really need to see if there is a reaction from him when he hears my voice.

I'm furious, seething, boiling inside with pent up anger and hatred for this man. I look him straight in the eye as I speak very eloquently, as I always do, he nods and gives that generic smile. He agrees with me this time, he should have done that months ago instead of ridiculing me live on television. Then he could have saved us both a lot of grief, but damn it, he doesn't remember me.

I console myself with the thought of how clever and cunning I have been over the last few months. There have been moments when I've been watching him going about his life. I was concerned he may have noticed me on more than one occasion. Of course that's inconceivable. My surveillance skills are second to none. I've had years and countless people who I chose to monitor, to perfect my skills.

Over the years I've written to many security agencies including the government's MI5 and MI6, but the bastards never reply. If they knew what I was capable of they would take me seriously and realise my worth. This country needs more people like me!

The show, if that is what you can call it, yes that's exactly what it is, has come to an end. He's left the studio with his guest panel, he didn't give me a second glance. That's okay by me because when he next looks into my face, he will be pleading for his life. With that thought in my mind, I really can't help it, a smile spreads across my face as I leave the studio.

What the, who's grabbing my arm? I'm shaken from my reverie as I walk along the corridor; two policemen have a hold on me. They take me to a side room and it appears they are arresting me! Stalking, vandalism, threatening letters, this is ridiculous. They have no idea how badly he has treated me. This will all be explained when we get to the police station and then they will realise how all my actions have been justified.

As I’m sat in the back of the police car, I’m feeling very pleased with myself. He did recognise and acknowledge me after all.

So until we meet again, and oh yes we will!

INJUSTICE

It's not right, it wasn't my fault. She looked at the letter from the courts. A restraining order forbidding her to make contact with her five year old daughter.

He looks at his young daughter. He knows her mother would never hurt her. However, she had attacked him, badly enough to put him in hospital.

The plan had worked, she had taken the husband and the child from the woman she despised. He succumbed to her flattery. Some intimate photos sent to that woman's phone has succeeded in sending her into a rage and attacking her dearly beloved.

Sweet revenge.

HOMELESS

We sit watching the strangers passing by, busy with their lives. Wrapped up against the cold wind that is whipping down the street. We have some food and we huddle together, not only to keep warm, but because it feels good. Some comfort in an inhospitable world. How did we get here you may ask? It could be my fault, though my friend says I saved him, that day. He found me drowning in the river, my four legs tied. He was there to throw himself in. It's getting dark, time to find a safe place to sleep.

THE NEIGHBOUR

My god it's freezing out here, but I'm determined I will learn to focus this contraption. Maybe I didn't read the instructions properly, there wouldn't be any surprise there, I have to admit. I'm the type of person who unpacks whatever, switches it on and expects it to work perfectly first time.

Right one more try and then I'm going to pack up and go inside and make myself a hot drink. Shame though it's such a clear starlit night, I should be able to get a good view of at least one planet.

Oh…, what was that? Shit I could get in trouble here, the neighbours might think I'm spying on them. I just looked right into their bedroom. Now if I move over to the left, I'm sure Saturn should be in that direction. My god, did I really just see that, it was so quick. I'm not sure what to do, so I pack up my telescope and step through the door into my cosy warm kitchen. Saturn and its rings will have to wait for my observations on another night.

Sipping my hot chocolate, the image of what I saw keeps flashing back at me. Lovely old Albert my neighbour, bludgeoning his horrible wife Irene to death!

I never liked her but I'm not alone there. Irene never has a nice word to say about anyone. From what I've heard she has made Albert's life a misery. Even their daughters moved abroad to get away from her. One to Singapore the other New Zealand, You couldn't go much further than that could you?

Walking my dog the next day, his name is Buster by the way, there's Albert cleaning his car, whistling away to himself. He sees me and lifts his hand in a wave, I wave back. I cannot imagine that gentle looking old hand striking a deadly blow. But then again the victim was Irene.

I'm quite positive now I've been thinking about it on and off since last night, I have to believe what I saw. Now here is the dilemma, what do I do? Then again I could be wrong, part of me hopes I'm not, I couldn't abide the woman. With more than one run in with her over the years, and poor Albert always trying to be the peacemaker, only for her to turn her wrath on to him. Do I really want to inform the police and him serve a life sentence, because that is what it would amount to at his age, the answer I give myself is no. I'm surprised he hasn't done it sooner and anyway in my eyes it's a case of justifiable homicide, and I've watched enough programs on crime, real and fictitious, to validate my opinion.

It's been a couple of weeks now, apparently Irene has gone to New Zealand to see their Michelle. Now if this is true, it's quite odd to say the least because Irene has always been terrified of flying, everyone who knew her, knew that. Albert would have loved to go abroad for his holidays to see the kids but she had refused to fly. I'm thinking, knowing what I know, I wish Albert had thought of something more plausible to tell the neighbours.

A few days later I'm driving back from the shops, turning into the road where I live and there in front of Albert's house are two police cars. He is being led away in handcuffs. As I drive slowly past trying to take in the scene, Albert looks straight at me and winks.

I should feel sad for him, but I think the wink he gave me, says he will be okay. The life sentence he will probably serve is far better than the one he was already doing.

ONLY ONE WISH

It had been a boring and argumentative Saturday morning for the twins. Nine year old Sid and Nancy had nothing to do but get on each other's nerves. They both resented the fact they had to share the few meagre toys, some of which were broken anyway. They both blamed each other, when asked by their weary worn father, who was responsible while he reminded them yet again there was no money to replace them.

The family was in what is called the poverty trap. Mum had deserted them years before, becoming thoroughly tired of the constant penny pinching. The twins couldn't remember what she looked like and their Dad certainly didn't want to, even if there were any photos of her displayed around the squalid council house. Life had been hard and Les had done his best on his low wage to provide for his children. The family had now resorted to going to the local food bank for their groceries.

The morning had been made worse by the fact it had not stopped raining, so the twins couldn't even go outside. Dad had promised them if the rain cleared up they could go along to the travelling fair. The only problem was he only had two pounds each to give them. It was all he could spare and the sad look on his face as he put the coins into their hands, told so many stories of which the twins would never be aware.

Just after midday the rain finally stopped and the sun made intermittent appearances, typical of the english summer. At least now the twins could escape the confines of the house and their poor beleaguered father could have some peace for a while.

Shutting the door behind them, Sid and Nancy skipped down the garden path and off down the road to the local park where the travelling fair had set up camp.

They were both hoping to sneak on some of the rides without paying while the attendants were not looking, or busy taking money from the fee paying public. They wanted to get hot dogs with their money.

As they ran down the road, Sid deliberately jumped in the puddles left by the morning rain; when Nancy moved quickly away so she wouldn't get splashed, he started kicking his feet in the puddles, so then she retaliated. By the time they got to the fair, their shoes and jeans were soaked. Oblivious to this they joined the queue at the hotdog stand, then wandered around for a bit amongst the rides and the crowds. They had attempted to get on a couple of the amusement rides, however, the fairground operators were to savvy and chased them off.

Walking around aimlessly, there wasn't a lot they could do with the fifty pence each, they now had left. Neither of them really wanted to be with the other, but both incapable of shunning the unconscious security of the others presence.

Then they both spotted a sign 'MAGIC WISH PEBBLES FOR SALE 50p' The twins made a beeline for the stall. The rather weaselly looking man who was selling the pebbles, took their money and instructed them to hold them tightly in the palm of their hands, and make a wish. Make it wisely he told them, with a sly look in his eye, there was only one wish each!

Eager to get away from the man as they both found him a bit scary, they ran over to a large oak tree which seemed as good a place as any to make a wish. Standing there under the tree, their feet balancing on the exposed roots,

Sid and Nancy looked nervously and uncertainly at each other. The wind had suddenly picked up and was whipping around the tree. They shivered and both started to cry a little, then they squeezed their pebbles in their hands and each made a wish. Unbeknown to each other, they each felt there was a strange feeling of nothingness.

How could they know they would both make the same wish. That neither of them wanted to be a twin and wanted the other to simply not be there!

A young mum passed by the tree pushing her baby in a pram. She could have sworn she saw two stones or pebbles suddenly drop to the ground from nowhere. How strange is that she thought and walked on by.

THE CHASE

Did I black out or what? I must have fainted. Where the hell am I? Patrick looked up at the blue cloudless sky. Closing his fists he could feel sand escaping through his fingers. Then he became aware of the sound of waves lapping onto the beach. He tentatively moved his arms and legs, and gently turned his head from side to side. I don't appear to be injured, he thought, no pain.

'I've found him, he's over here.' A male voice coming closer.

'Is he alive?' Someone else shouted.

'Not now.' He replied as he pulled the trigger.

DISCOVERY

She is not dead, she can't be dead. It's not possible, she is just in a deep sleep. Her body is still warm and soft. The scent of her filling my nostrils. I should phone someone, an ambulance. No, there's no need, she's not dead. What a stupid idea, pull yourself together, she thought to herself. Don't get hysterical, she's not dead. Then why don't you pick her up? She told herself. I can't do that, what if she feels limp in my arms. Then she must be dead and that is unthinkable. Picking up her baby girl, she sobs.

FACE AT THE WINDOW

Sitting in the local coffee shop, Chrissie had chosen the table nearest the window. With her hands wrapped around her coffee cup she liked to watch the passers by going about their business. Some hurrying like they had not a moment to lose, others in groups absorbed in conversations and not paying any attention to the other people having to make detours around them. Old folk carefully walking along avoiding any raised flags on the footpaths, that would invariably result in a broken hip.

She suddenly becomes aware of a man who has stopped directly outside the window, staring straight at her. A sharp intake of breath and she is immediately and unwillingly taken back fifty two years, when she was eight years old.

There is nothing similar or familiar about the man standing there, except she thought him quite rude for staring. Perhaps she shouldn't be so judgemental maybe he had mental health issues or is very short sighted, he wasn't wearing glasses. He's a middle aged man and not particularly attractive looking, so not her knight in shining armour, she was waiting for to come into her life. Obviously middle aged wasn't a problem, she was no spring chicken herself. However, she had always taken great care with her appearance and had certain standards; this man did not match up to them. Therefore she gave him the look which indicated *not interested, go away*. He read it right and with the suggestion of a wink, he walked on.

Chrissie watched him walk away as her thoughts turned back to the night many years ago, when she had seen another man's face staring at her, through the kitchen window of her family home. Home maybe not quite the word to describe it, the place they lived was a better description. They being her mum, dad, and herself and her younger brother Andy, only younger by fourteen months. However, this didn't stop her mum heaping the responsibility of him onto Chrissie at every opportunity. She never resented her brother for this, she loved him! They were more than siblings, they were *comrades in arms* supporting each other as best they could in their young lives. Left to their own devices most of the time. Both parents worked then spent their money drinking in the local pubs. The children didn't like being left on their own every night, but of course were powerless to change anything. So each night they were given instructions not to answer the door to anybody, ever!

The winter nights were by far the worst. The darkness that descended not long after they were home from school, seemed to surround the house. Harbouring all manner of things that could be conjured up in the minds of two fearful and anxious children. To make matters worse, the kitchen window only had some very tired looking net curtains, which only came half way up the window, *cafe style* is how they would be described now. It was over the top of these Chrissie saw the face looking in, when she had gone into the kitchen to get her and Andy a drink. Needless to say neither of them got the drinks as she screamed and ran back into the living room. Andy who had been curled up in the old armchair watching *Sunday Night at the London Palladium,* on their little black and white tv, jumped up.

'What is it?' He said looking alarmed

Seeing the fear on his face she, not only because she was older and always felt responsible for his welfare; she forced a smile and said.

‘Horrible big spider in the kitchen sink.’

Andy knew his sister was terrified of spiders and he didn’t like them either. So Chrissie was sure he wouldn’t offer to deal with it. Nevertheless the man was still out there. Would he try to get in, what does he want, what would happen if he got in? All of these questions going round in her head.

It was then she heard a rattling noise, was he trying the back door? Then of course the next big question, did he know they were on their own? Fear was threatening to overtake her, yet even for her young years she knew she must keep it together and not panic.

Then came the earth shattering scream, both children startled, looked into each other’s faces.

‘What was that?’ Said Andy whilst launching himself from the chair he had been sat in, over to Chrissie’s arms.

She held him tight, but couldn’t stop her own body trembling, holding back the tears welling up in her eyes.

‘A fox,’ she stuttered ‘I think it’s a fox.’

Holding Andy close and rubbing his back the way she had seen grownups do when they were comforting someone. Her first thought was, would they have heard that up at the farm? That was the nearest home to their *tied* cottage, where they lived because their dad was the head farmhand. Both her and Andy loved being around the farm. Mr and Mrs Finney who owned the farm were very kind to them. Their two daughters, they had no sons; were grown up now and had never shown any interest in the farm. Quite the opposite, they had both moved to London to be part of the ‘*Swinging Sixties*. Chrissie could not understand it, she loved the fields and the animals and not least the delicious pies and cakes, Mrs Finney baked. She knew their mum never baked, preferring to work at the local and in fact the only ladies shop in the village.

We have to get out of here, Crissie thought. It could be hours before either mum or dad came back. She so desperately wanted the safety of the cosy farmhouse.

'Right Andy.' She said, quickly formulating a story that would be believable to her seven year old brother.

'We need to go and tell Mr Finney about the fox, just in case he hasn't locked all the chickens in the hen house. Do you remember the last time the fox got them?'

'Yes.' He said putting on his serious face. 'Blood and guts everywhere.'

'That's right.' Said Chrissie, trying to contain the panic rising up inside her, so much so she thought she may be sick. 'But let's make it an adventure.'

Looking straight into Andy's baby blue eyes, she got both of his hands in hers, hoping this would convey to him, but not panic him they must act quickly and get away from the house, without being seen. Chrissie was hoping the man and whoever else was out there were still round the back of the house. The front door was round the side, they couldn't risk going out that way, so the only other option was out through the living room window at the front.

'Okay Andy, follow me we are going to climb through the window.'

'Are we?' Said Andy. A little bit of excitement but also nervousness in his voice. He didn't want to get in trouble with mum and dad when they got back. It wouldn't be the first time Chrissie had got them into trouble, but that's another story.

‘Yes it’s alright, don’t worry.’

The brother and sister were so close sometimes they could tune into each other almost telepathically. She knew what he was thinking.

‘Mum and dad won’t shout. Come on now.’ she said as she pulled back one side of the curtains.

The blackness outside was all enveloping, apart from a few visible stars and a quarter moon that did little to break the darkness.

Climbing up onto the window ledge and opening the window, Chrissie senses heightened, ears straining for any sound of approaching footsteps. She scanned the front garden for any sign of movement, nothing! Her heart pounding so hard she was sure not only would Andy hear it, but whoever else was out there. She lowered herself down into the garden, scraping her knees down the wall, jumping may make too much noise. Reaching her hand up through the window, graspings Andy’s hand, she put her fingers to her lips to gesture for him to be quiet. At that point she realised the light from the living room and the noise from the television, may alert whoever was out there. With this thought in her head, she practically dragged Andy through the window and he landed a bit harder and louder than she would have liked. As soon as his feet made contact with the ground she started running pulling her brother alongside her, they sprinted through the garden gate and towards the farmhouse.

‘Can I take this cup?’ Said the young man; dish cloth in one hand, tray in the other.

‘Oh yes.’ She said, suddenly coming back into the present day. Glancing around she realised the place had got quite full and his request was also a hint the table was needed. Picking up her bag from the side of her chair, she looked again at the young man. His name badge said Andy. With a slight catch in her breath as she stood up, she said “Thank you Andy.”

With that she walked out of the coffee shop, those memories of long ago were still acting out in her head. No longer able to share them with her brother, he had died many years ago.

When the two children had reached the farmhouse there were no lights on downstairs, but thankfully a light was glowing from an upstairs window. Breathing a sigh of relief, Chrissie was relieved that Mr and Mrs Finney were still up.

Hammering on the door, Chrissie was also calling. ‘Mrs Finney, Mr Finney please let us in.’ She heard heavy footsteps on the wooden stairs and then the deadbolt being slid back on the door. It opened wide and there stood Mr Finney, a giant of a man or so he seemed to the two children. They didn’t wait to be asked in but pushed past the startled farmer. Andy was now realising there was more to the flight from their house, than the imminent risk to the farm chickens, from any fox!

‘What on earth is going on?’ Said Mrs Finney, as she came down the stairs fastening the buttons of her quilted dressing gown around her ample middle. At that point Chrissie burst into tears, Andy turned to her and put his arms around her as his eyes started to well up.

‘Oh lovey, what has happened, have you hurt yourselves?’ She wrapped her arms round both of the children. She looked over at her husband with concern and bafflement in her eyes.

‘Warm up some hot milk Reg, these children are chilled to the bone.’

'Aye alright, bit of a rum do this is. It's nearly half ten they should be tucked up in their own beds now.'

'Never mind about that now, there's something very wrong here. Come and sit down next to the fire children and you tell Auntie Mae what's happened.'

As the children sipped their hot chocolate and watched Mr Finney stoke up the fire, Chrissie related the events that had led them to flee to the farmhouse. Andy hearing the full story for the first time looked at his sister, his mouth dropping open.

'Right,' said Mr Finney. 'I'm going down to the village and get Bert Simmons.' Bert was the one man police force at the time; 'and I'll call in the Dog and Partridge, that's more than likely where Sally and Bill will be, I'll tell them to come and collect their kids.'

Mae could tell from his tone of voice, he would be having a word with the both of them, about leaving their young children alone at night.

With that he pulled on his big coat and flat cap on his head.

'Bolt the door after me Mae, I'll be back as quick as I can.'

*****

The next morning all had become evident. A young local woman, eighteen year old Samantha Hooper had been found partially buried on the land at the back of the children's house. Killed by a blow to the head from a large rock, it turned out she had also been raped; this latter bit of information whispered quietly around the shocked residents of the usually quiet country village.

Samantha had been drinking in the local pub with a man nobody recognised, but could give a good description of him. Luckily he was known to the county police for the attempted rape of another woman. Unfortunately no charges were ever brought against him as it was her word against his. In those days the police were not as sympathetic or pro-active as they are now.

The man was arrested later that day, at the home he shared with his wife and two young sons.

Just a few nights later, sitting by the dwindling fire, Andy said to Chrissie.

'Has that bad man been locked up now?'

'Yes he has.' Said Chrissie.

'So he won't come and get us?'

'No he won't, don't worry I'm here.' She said, not feeling as confident as she was trying to sound, and wishing with all her heart, mum and dad would have carried on staying at home with them, as they had done for the last few weeks since the murder.

But normal service had been resumed.

BROKEN RELATIONSHIPS

I can't think what I will do without Anton. Such a tragic accident, it should never have happened. I was so dependent on him, he was the caretaker of my life never far from my side.

That day I hadn't been paying much attention to him, I wonder if he felt I was neglecting him. If we were to be separated, life could prove very difficult for me.

I did my utmost to revive him, but he was too far gone. Oh well, I'm off to the phone shop again, another one dropped down the toilet.

C'est la vie!

JUST ANOTHER DAY AT WORK

I noticed Darren muttering to himself, nothing unusual in that, he did it all the time. I kind of got used to him. We had been renovating this old house for about a month now. I hadn't worked with him before; the boss seemed to think it was a good idea to pair us up. Darren appeared okay at first but each day we worked on the house, he got more agitated. The next minute he's got the pickaxe in his hand demolishing the rear cellar wall. From the hole he made, came the stench of rotting flesh.

THE DAY SHE FORGOT

The phone rings startling her, she wipes the tears from her eyes and thinks I can't deal with one of those annoying cold calls right now. But she picks up the phone anyway, there's a silence at first and just as she is about to put the phone down, a female voice says.

'I know what you have done.'

'What, who is this?' She replies.

The phone goes silent, the caller has hung up. She holds the phone in her hands for a few seconds, shakes her head and puts it back on the receiver.

Looking around her large airy kitchen, her eyes are red and swollen from the last hour or so of sobbing. Just how desolate can a person feel and still carry on? She thinks. And what on earth was that phone call about, was it simply a wrong number? The voice she heard already fading from her thought processes, it wasn't menacing or threatening, nor even accusing in it's tone. Just a statement!

What could I have possibly done? She thinks. Oh this is just stupid, in the great scheme of things, why should a phone call bother her. It probably wasn't even meant for her, but nevertheless she feels uneasy. There's something tapping away at the back of her mind, as if she didn't have enough to think about.

She looks at the clock on the wall, almost six o'clock, he will be in from work soon. She has no intention of giving him the satisfaction of seeing how upset she is, by his devastating news. This, he had decided to break to her yesterday, while they were out on their usual Sunday walk. She hurries upstairs to repair the damage to her makeup, always conscious of how she looks, wanting to look her best not just for him but for herself. She's not bad looking for her age and kept her figure more or less. There has not been any childbearing to do any damage, and although her body no longer aches to carry a child; her heart still pines in a quiet way for what could have been.

There that's much better, looking at her reflection in the mirror, as she gently dabs the puffy eyes with powder foundation. Already having spent a few minutes splashing cold water onto her face.

Now downstairs back in the kitchen, it's going to be cold meat and salad tonight, it's been a warm stuffy day. If he thinks she was going to have the oven on cooking for him today, well he can forget it he's lucky to get the salad!

Seven o'clock, where is he? Good job she didn't cook, it would be ruined by now! He is such an inconsiderate man, not even a call to say he would be late. Then her heart sinks and her stomach knots. Of course he's with her now, how stupid could she be and as the tears well up in her eyes again, she remembers she slept alone last night. He must have slept in the spare room and by the time she woke up this morning he had already left for work, without even a goodbye. She should hate and despise him but she doesn't, she loves him. She has since the first day she clapped eyes on him. Her brother four years her senior had introduced them at a friend's wedding. For her there would never be anyone else, and even after thirty two years of marriage, she still felt as passionate about him.

*****

She opens her eyes and reaches out to turn off the alarm clock on the bedside table. It's not the alarm, the phone is ringing! She lets out a deep sigh, reaching over his side of the bed; he's not there. Her mind is clouded and groggy, was she drinking last night? She picks up the phone still leaning on his side of the bed, she can faintly smell his cologne.

'Hello.' She says a little abruptly.

'I know what you have done.' The voice says.

'Who are you, what the hell are you talking about?'

There's no response, nothing but silence. This is just ridiculous she thinks, I'm going to report these calls to the phone company. Still holding the phone she realizes she didn't close the curtains the night before, so the early morning sun is streaming through the window. Then another revelation she's still wearing her clothes from the night before. She can't remember actually coming to bed. What state was she in she wonders, and then the reality hits her, he didn't come home last night.

Making her way downstairs, still in yesterday's clothes, hair dishevelled from an apparently restless night and most of her makeup deposited on her pillow; she makes herself a strong cup of coffee and sits down at the kitchen table, head in hands.

What do I do now? She thinks to herself, what are those damned phone calls about. She hasn't done anything, she is the innocent party in all of this. Maybe it's her, the other woman, what has he been saying to her?

She lifts her head up from the kitchen table, disorientated, she must have fell asleep again. Looking at the clock it's nearly ten, the doorbell is ringing. Maybe it's him, no it can't be he has a key! Wearily she gets up to answer the door, forgetting momentarily her unaccustomed appearance until she answers the door, embarrassed but then frozen on the spot at the sight of two police officers on her doorstep.

The policewoman introduces herself and her male colleague and asks if the can come in.

'What's happened, has he had an accident, is he okay?' Her voice trembling and full of trepidation.

'Sit down please,' says the female officer. 'Is there anyone else in the house with you?'

'No,' she replies, 'just me.'

'We have to inform you, a body has been found at the bottom of Lark Fell Quarry, from the wallet found, we believe the man could be your husband. We are very sorry but we need you to come to the mortuary to identify him.'

'What happened, how did he?' Her voice trails away at that point as she looks at them beseechingly.

'We can't say for sure at the moment.' Says the male officer.

'I need to put some shoes on, just give me a minute.'

Upstairs she hurriedly applies some makeup and attempts to do something with her hair.

'What have they just said?' She mutters to herself.

Then the phone rings, and she picks it up.

'They know what you have done.'

Who? She thinks. The police? I haven't done anything, I'm sure I haven't. This is madness it's not going to be him, they have made a mistake.

It’s not a mistake, there he is lying there on the mortuary slab, his body cold and empty. She wants to touch him but she’s afraid. His skin looks waxy but bruised as well from the fall that has killed him.

‘Yes that’s my husband.’ She says without looking at the police officer standing by her side.

Then she knows with agonising certainty, as the room starts spinning around her and she crumples to the floor. She killed him!

In the soft interview room where she has been taken, she cries inconsolably and with resignation recounts the events that led up to her husband’s death.

They had set out on their usual walk on Sunday. The tension between them had been building for months. Her suspicions finally proved when he admitted he was having an affair. That was bad enough, she wanted to scream and punch and hurt him. But then he dealt her the final unforgivable blow. He was leaving her because the other woman was having his child. With a primeval scream that she didn’t even recognise was coming from her, she turned and pushed him with such force and strength she never knew she had. She kept pushing him until he slipped on the loose ground at the edge of the quarry, and then he fell!

She doesn’t remember how she got home, not in the car, he had the car keys. The next thing she can recall is sitting in her kitchen when the phone rings. At that point it comes to her there was no one on the phone, no phone calls. It was her conscience not pricking but stabbing her to acknowledge the utter devastation that had taken place on the day she had forgot!

CONFRONTATION

Here he comes, such a cocky dude, throwing his weight around. Okay I will admit he's impressive and maybe in another life, I may be born into a physique like that. It's certainly not going to happen in this lifetime, but give me a break! I was here first, he thinks he can just push us little guys around. Well I'm not standing for it, this will be my moment to make my stand. The Mrs will be impressed when I tell her, or maybe not, the robin thought, as the magpie swooped down for the mealworms.

RECOLLECTIONS

I know that man. I'm sure I know him he thought as they passed by each other, eyes making contact but no recognition from the passer by. He limped home slowly, his walking was getting better and stronger. The car accident nearly two years ago had dramatically changed his life. Severe head injuries, they didn't think he would live. Months of rehabilitation in hospital. Then an image flashes across his mind. The paramedic he had just seen was opening his car door.

'Don't worry mate, we will get you out.'

Just as he stopped breathing for the first time.

DOG FOUND IN POSSESSION OF A SECURITY TAG

Dog warden Chris Bailey, came across a peculiar site while doing his round in a borough of Stockport last week. Mr Bailey had parked his van near the entrance to a local park. It was a pleasant summer morning, hopefully it would not get to hot later on he thought, but certainly a good day for all the kids on the start of the summer holidays.

As he turned off the engine on his van, he became aware of a group of excited children, looked like seven in all, all ranging from six to eight years old. They could be heard laughing and shouting whilst chasing a Jack Russell dog, near the entrance to the park. Which in turn, the dog was barking excitedly and obviously enjoying the chase.

Chris got out of the van to investigate, because in that particular park the sign at the entrance clearly stated. 'DOGS MUST BE ON LEADS AT ALL TIMES'. As he was approaching the children he called out to them to stop chasing the dog! The startled children, who amongst all the mayhem had not been aware of his presence, came to a standstill almost like a game of musical statues, and comically so did the dog.

On enquiring who the dog belonged to? The children looked at him with a mixture of amusement and apprehension. None of them knew but they thought they had seen the dog a few times in the park, but it didn't seem to have an owner.

They said they were trying to catch him and he had something strange around his neck. The dog meanwhile was wagging it's tail enthusiastically, appeared to want to carry on with chase. Chris hunched down and whistled to the dog, which came running to him in a friendly manner. He held his hand out for it to sniff and got the surprise of his life when he saw the dog was wearing a security tag around its neck.

On closer inspection, although the tag was not fastened it had somehow got attached to the dogs collar. Chris removed the tag so he could get a proper look at the collar, for a name and phone number. A smile spread across his face on reading the dogs name was 'Ripper'. Somebody had an ironic sense of humour. Other than that there was no other information on who the dog's owner might be. So the next best option was the security tag, which may or may not belong to the owner.

It turned out the tag belonged to a twenty year old man by the name of Dwayne Goose. He was on a charge for receiving stolen goods.

Some weeks later during his court appearance, Mr Goose claimed his dog Ripper must have chewed through the tag while he was asleep and managed to get it around its neck. He then further claimed he didn't notice the next morning when he went to let the dog out, that instead of it being around his ankle, Ripper was now wearing it!

Dwayne's house backs onto the park and Ripper was a frequent visitor there.

Mr Goose was ordered by Judge Armstrong not to breach his curfew again, with or without the aid of his dog.

Ripper was returned to his owner on a lead but not tagged!

TODAY

The alarm goes off, its 4am he drags himself out of bed unable to get out of his old routine. He knows there are no longer any cows to milk. They have all been sold off, he couldn't afford the upkeep anymore. The supermarkets had been squeezing him on his prices, constantly wanting him to supply the milk cheaper than before. Too many creditors snapping at his heels, and now the landowner wants him off the farm. His family had been tenants here for six generations. He knows he should have bought it years ago before the previous landowners had sold on. It was a good price they had been willing to let him have it for, and Beth the Mrs said at the time it would secure the future for their two sons Tom and George. If only he had done that! At least he could have sold some of the land to the ever present predatory land developers, looking to build their luxury executive homes; on this green and pleasant land.

He walks down the stairs heading for the kitchen. The house is very quiet, they are all in their beds. He doesn't sleep with the Mrs anymore, what with all the arguing over the last few months. Yes he knows its all his fault, but he doesn't need her constantly reminding him. It was getting harder and harder for him to control his anger with her. The lads don't give him respect anymore, always taking their mother's side.

'Well you run the bloody farm.' He would shout at them. 'You're almost men! I was working at your age, not staying on at bloody school. Doing business management and all that rubbish!' He would say bitterly, but he knew in his heart of hearts if he had more business sense, this farm may have survived. Times had moved on since his dad worked the farm; the problem was he was still working the way things had always been done. He wasn't a man for negotiating the prices of his dairy products with the supermarkets. He is an insular man more comfortable with the land than the people who inhabit it.

In the kitchen now he puts the kettle on for a mug of tea and opens the fridge; no milk, how ironic! In fact there isn't much of anything. Today has got to be the day, this can't go on. He doesn't want to go down to the village shop anymore and face the questions. He's told that nosey Pam who works part time in there, *they have gone to family for a few weeks.* Well he had to say something.

Pulling a chair out and sitting down heavily at the kitchen table, he swats a fly from his face. They are buzzing around the kitchen adding to his misery.

'Yes.' he says startling himself, by saying it out loud. 'Today is the day.'

Then he reaches out for the shotgun leaning against the kitchen table. He puts the barrel end of the gun in his mouth and pulls the trigger, as the unspoken words in his head say. *Sod it.*

Upstairs in their respective bedrooms oblivious to his final act, lay the month old corpses of what were his family. Shot to death whilst asleep in their beds, and in his tormented mind with love and determination it was the only way he could see to solve their problems.

THE JOB

How did it go? He asked me. It was said in such a casual manner, he could have been asking me, how the weather was on my holiday.

He had hired me to abduct his wife, take her in the early hours of the morning to her lover's apartment. Forcing her lover at gunpoint to stab her to death. He was crying and pleading with me. He said he was getting bored with her anyway. Those words from him gave me some job satisfaction as I instructed him to put the gun to his head.

Job done, I told him.

GROSS NEGLIGENCE

I tried to warn them, they were making all the wrong decisions just to save some costs. They being the owners of the yet to be built, private nursing home. The problem was all they could see were the profits to be made.
I had to resign as the project manager, thank god I did. Though of course I feel desperately sorry for all those frail old folks who perished in the building collapse.

I stand here now in court, giving my evidence.

TIME DOESN'T PLAY FAIR

You know that old adage *time is a great healer*, well yes it can be. However, time does lots of other things as well.

For instance time plays tricks, deluding you into thinking there is more of it than you can actually have. This can produce feelings of panic and the belief that the task in hand will never be completed.

The appointment you are going to miss, so you risk driving over the speed limit and then what happens? You get caught on that damned speed camera. Of course the advice frequently given is. *Allow plenty of time for your journey.* This is very good in theory, if time would just give you a few more hours in the day.

Then there's the time device on the wall in the exam room, the clock. The already nervous students furtively glancing at it now and again; it imposes feelings of anxiety and tension looking through the questions on the examination papers. Plagued by the thoughts of impending failure, all those laborious hours of revision time in vain.

What about the time sat in waiting rooms? Doctors, dentists, hospitals, when taken into consideration you would be much happier being anywhere else. The GP surgery is running late again. The A&E department has as a big sign, at least a four hour wait, oh well there's always the vending machine and the tv on the wall to keep you going, oh the joy. Needless to say who in their right mind wants to spend time at the dentists?

Of course let's not forget what time does to our visage and anatomy. There's the reminder when we look in the mirror, while we slap on the latest wonder time-delay cream. Your thinking, will this one actually work and if you apply it more generously will it be more effective? That is something to ponder on but you can't not use it, because what would you look like then? Heaven forbid.

Time sat in the crowded airport lounge, closely monitoring your flight details on the information board and oh no, your flight is delayed. So one more walk around the duty free shops, to pass a bit more time. Maybe another coffee, at this rate you will be so high on caffeine you could fly there yourself.

Then there is the precious time which definitely doesn't play fair. While you cling onto the very moment not wanting to move on; holding the hand and weeping for the loved one fading away.

Frustrating time spent in traffic holdups.

Endless time queueing for the supermarket checkout.

Time spent wasting time.

Wishing we had our time again.

Desperate for it to slow down in the good times and speed through the tough ones.

Try as you might you can't control it, but with determination you make the most of it.

If you only had a bit more time.

GREEN FINGERS

What made him think he could ever get away with this? The whole thing was becoming a nightmare for him. Only yesterday despite his best efforts of concealment, he couldn't control the wildlife and he had chased that fox away three times now.

Then Eric from next door had called round to ask could he have some compost for his roses. He would bring his wheelbarrow round if that was okay? Christ almighty, Ted thought, he knew he had offered many a time to the neighbours they could help themselves to his small mountain of compost, but now!

'Leave me your wheelbarrow Eric, I'm doing some reorganising in the garden today, I'll bring it round shortly.'

'Right you are, I'll have the kettle on, you've got time for a cuppa haven't you?' Replied Eric.

With that he walked back down Ted's driveway.

Ted closed the door, luckily no one was there to witness his shaking and sweating.

*****

Six Months Earlier...

'While you out in the village Sylvia, will you check the ads in the paper shop, and see if anyone is looking to do some gardening work.'

'Why can't you look?' Sylvia said in an indignant tone.

‘Because.’ He said in a long drawn patronising way, ‘As you very well know, I’m meeting the lads for a game of golf.’

‘Lads,’ she scoffed ‘your just a bunch of middle aged men knocking a ball around, with sticks, in a field full of holes.’

Later that day over dinner, Sylvia informed Ted she had in fact found them a gardener. A very nice young man who had just set up his own business, after working for his dad for a few years.

But was he any good Ted had asked. Sylvia smiled, she actually didn’t care. With him in the garden, she would have a renewed interest in gardening.

Nathan came round the following week, on Ted’s golf day. Sylvia had told Ted it was the only day he had free at the moment. Not strictly true but Ted had accepted that, with a comment he would be inspecting the lad’s work when he got back from golf. On hearing this comment Sylvia had a little smile to herself. Bidding her husband goodbye for a few hours, she went up to the bathroom to shave her legs and any other parts that needed attention.

Nathan’s fortnightly visits proved very satisfactory for both Ted and Sylvia. Ted had said on more than one occasion it would be nice for him to meet Nathan as he was doing an exceptional job with the garden. Another plus was Sylvia was giving him an easier life, not picking on all his idiosyncrasies. She was even cooking his favourite meal for him, fish pie, when he came home from golf.

But all good things eventually end, and that was the day the golf was cancelled due to the sudden demise of Adrian, one of Ted’s golf buddies. Ted had turned up at the golf club at the usual time, but none of the lads were there. He went into the club, thinking he would get a coffee while he was waiting for them. The barman Barry, who was a most unlikeable character, god knows how he got the job, the members would say, seemed surprised to see him. It turns out an email had been sent out to Adrian's cohortes, saying the golf was cancelled. Ted never read his emails, he was of the firm belief a phone was for talking on and that is what he used it for!

When Ted got home, Nathan's van was on the drive parked next to Sylvia's car, but there was no sight or sound of Nathan. That was until Ted entered the hallway of his house to be greeted by the sounds from upstairs. The pleasurable moans of his wife and the grunts and groans of the athletically built gardener. Ted then walked out of the house and sat in his car.

Sometime later Nathan made an appearance, having casually closed the front door behind him, he sauntered over to his van. That was when Ted got out of his car and informed him his services would no longer be required. Without argument but with a smirk on his face, Nathan got in his van and drove off.

Sylvia was still in their bed, when Ted entered the room. The bed was in disarray and so was Sylvia's hair as Ted struck her repeatedly about the head with the garden mallet!

THE VAN

‘That van is still there.’

‘Yes,’ he replied, ‘it’s been there for weeks now, somebody needs to report it.’

The couple walked towards the rusting white van, left abandoned in the layby. It was as if there was some sort of screen cover on the windscreen.

‘Do you see that Joyce, what is it?’

‘I don’t know Fred, but it looks like it’s moving.’

As they got up close, they could both see a mass of flies on the inside of the windscreen.

Just a fraction of the many thousand feeding off the corpse inside the van.

DINNER DATE

A handsome couple sat opposite each other in their beautiful Orangery. The table was set for six places, four friends invited. The setting was immaculate, designer crockery and wine glasses, solid silver cutlery. A gorgeous arrangement of fresh cut flowers, delivered from the local florist, adorned the centre of the table. The doorbell was ringing insistently, their guests had arrived. However, there was no attempt to open the door and let them in. The husband and wife staring blankly at each other. The patio doors are wide open where the assassin had entered, and swiftly slit both their throats.

MISGIVINGS

God it's a cold night, can't wait to get home. I don't like this public transport business but I only have myself to blame. The drinking just got out of control, I can see that now and I should count myself lucky I didn't lose my job as well as my license.

The wife has stuck by me in all of this and I'm very thankful for that. It does take me a lot longer now to get to work and back. Luckily to and from the nearest bus stop is this shortcut down the lane. It isn't great in the winter, it's dark and you never know if the dog walkers have cleaned up after their pooches.

Today though there is still some daylight left, the days are getting longer again, roll on spring and summer. *Hey what's going on up there? Looks like a fight.* Straining his eyes to see through the fading light he sees one person fall to the ground and the other is now running away further down the lane.

Oh my god! He breaks into a run to see if he can help. As he is running nearer to where he is sure he saw the incident, he can't see anyone on the ground or anyone around at all. What? I don't understand, he thinks. I couldn't have imagined that but there is definitely no one to be seen. Feeling uneasy and also a little stupid he continues his walk home. I'm not going to say anything to the wife, she might think I've been drinking again.

The evening passes quietly and normally, though he cannot get the scene of what he saw out of his mind.

I wonder, he thinks to himself, has he suffered some kind of brain damage from when he was drinking so heavily.

The next day the weather is cold but it's been sunny and very pleasant for February. As he gets off the bus to walk down the lane it's almost like spring. Not so many shadows today, he's says to himself in an almost comforting way. In fact he is not on his own as he can see a couple of dog walkers coming up the lane toward him. With a smile and a nod he passes the two ladies and their dogs. Walking a few more paces on he stops in his tracks, staring down at the ground in front of him. No it can't be, he thinks. They have just walked past with their dogs and they didn't even stop here. He shudders as he looks incredulously at the pool of blood on the ground, but even more horrifically at the sharp black handled kitchen knife lying in the sticky substance. What should I do, he questions himself. Then he hears footsteps coming towards him, thinking it is the dog walkers coming back to confirm what he is seeing.

'Are you okay mate?' The man says to him.

'No look.' He says as he takes his eyes away from the man to the mess on the ground.

'What mate?'

'I thought I saw something.' But now as he looks there is nothing there.

'Sorry.' He mumbles as he walks on, ignorant of the strange look he is getting from the passer by.

His wife is coming down the stairs as he lets himself into the house.

'Dom you look terrible, what's the matter are you ill?'

'I'm not feeling great, I might go straight to bed.'

'Shall I call the doctor?'

'No, just need to lie down for a while.'

'Alright, we will see how you feel in a bit. Go on up and I will bring you a cup of tea.'

Going into the bedroom he feels like his head is spinning. There must be something wrong with me. Am I going mad or is there a physiological reason for what is happening.

He sleeps badly that night and in the morning he momentarily considers phoning in sick. He can't though the boss has been really good to him, allowing him to keep his job, when some days he could barely switch on his computer.

I can't let him down he has been there for me. Although I do need to get a doctors appointment, this is really scaring me now.

It wasn't a great day at work. He got through it though and at least it's Friday, so hopefully, he was thinking he would feel much better after the weekend. A good rest that was what he needed.

Would you believe it! I just want to get home and the damned bus has broken down. It was another thirty minutes before another bus turned up to take the passengers on their way. By this time he was getting anxious, he knew by the time he got to his stop the lane would be in darkness. Don't be so stupid, he tells himself. You're a grown man.

When he finally arrives at his stop he is quite resolved he will not let his imagination get the better of him. I'm so tired, he thinks as he walks down the lane. Can't wait for a lie in tomorrow morning. Because it is dark now he is walking more carefully than usual to avoid stumbling over any obstacles such as fallen branches. The next minute he is grabbed from behind.

‘I’ve got a knife so don’t struggle.’ says the assailant. ‘Just give me your wallet and phone,’ he says in a low menacing tone. Then shouts ‘Now.’

He sees the glint of the knife bearing down on him. In a panic he makes a grab for the knife, taking the attacker by surprise. There is a struggle and as he turns to face the other man, he then he realises there is warm flowing blood all over his hand. He has stabbed his attacker in the abdomen. As he pulls the knife out, the man collapses. He drops the knife and it clatters to the ground. He takes a step back as the man reaches for the knife and attempts to get up. The next minute he is running away from his attacker. His heart pounding, running faster than he has ever done in his life. He runs blindly into the road, the oncoming car has no time to swerve and avoid him. He bounces over the car bonnet smashing into the windscreen, before he is tossed over the roof of the car, finally landing on the road. His sightless eyes stare up at the sky but there is no life in his mangled body.

ESCAPE TO THE COUNTRY

It was the fifth anniversary of their move from London to the country. Sylvia really hadn't wanted to move, but David her husband had insisted and David always got his own way, in the end. They had both taken early retirement at fifty five. Convenient some might have thought, them both being the same age.

Sylvia and David had met at university. It wasn't love at first sight or anything near that. It was more an acknowledgment of one another, that they were different from the other students. The pair of them both loners, almost socially inadequate. However, they were both driven by the need for success and recognition, even by those they deemed not worthy of their respect or time.

Success had come their way, David's in banking and Sylvia's in corporate law. There was never any time for family. They were both only children and they saw no advantage to keeping in touch with parents, or indeed procreating their own brood. With no friends as such, more acquaintances and work colleagues, their social life such as it was consisted mainly the two of them.

As an outsider looking at their lives there might be the misconception that they were happy and content to be with each other. In this you would be entirely wrong, Sylvia and David's fulfilments came completely from themselves. Despite this the marriage worked for both of them, it gave them an acceptable position in a society, they had never felt really part of. Two people in a marriage worked so much better for their selective careers, than two individuals who found social interaction extremely tedious but equally a necessity to further their careers.

Physically they were a mismatched couple. Sylvia a good deal taller than David and athletically built, she had maintained her strength and physique into her fifties. Apart from her career her other love in life was going to the gym. Whereas David had always been slightly built, he wasn't keen on any exercise and that also included the bedroom variety. On the odd occasion when the lift in their apartment building was out of service, and he had to use the stairs this would serve as an extreme annoyance to him. This he would convey to Sylvia throughout the evening, believing she was actually listening to him. It was to be Sylvia's good physical strength and stature that would enable her to eventually fulfil her plans.

The move to the country had been a source of heated arguments. In the end though Sylvia had conceded to her husband, though not for his benefit. She had to acknowledge to herself that at fifty five, she was becoming more and more invisible to the powers that be. The up and coming newbies in the world of corporate law were gradually moving her sideways, while they worked to promote their own careers. So Sylvia had decided it was time for her to move on and make her presence felt elsewhere.

In fact this is exactly what she had achieved in the village she now thought of as home. With the determination she had used in her work life, she quickly became head of the parish church committee, though she had absolutely no interest in religion. She was also on the board of governors for the local primary school, not for the benefit of the children of course, it was simply to feed her own ego. Also becoming the treasurer at the women's institute. She didn't do this for the comradeship, but simply to have the power over the other more malleable woman who didn't like to contradict her decisions.

Life was good and even better now she could live it on her own. After the move to the country, David had revealed he was in love with an ex work colleague Jason. He had moved back to London, that was the story anyway.

Sylvia sat on her decking, sipping a glass of red listening to the birds singing. A smile creeping across her face as she thought of David. Several feet under the new decking she had built. David mummified in several layers of heavy duty plastic sheeting, then taped up and wrapped again in tarpaulin, after caving in his skull with the garden spade. All those years at the gym had paid off, and she had actually enjoyed installing the decking.

David had simply become surplus to requirements.

UNFORESEEN CONSEQUENCES

She knew they were right of course. But she still couldn't grasp their point of view. There was the moral dilemma of it all. She hadn't meant any harm by her actions, things had gotten out of control. She wasn't malicious or vengeful, well not completely. She couldn't let people take advantage and walk all over her. When she started the fire, it was only to show them how it felt to have nothing, no home. That was the statement she gave the police. Nothing more to say.

A DESPERATE RESOLUTION

Once they had all agreed, the plans were put into action. Matters moved swiftly from there. However, some members of the government did raise their concerns. This was to be a huge undertaking the likes of which had never been done before. But this was the year 2040 and the economy of the country was in crisis. The population on long term benefits, had to be resolved drastically. All the facilities needed to sustain life would be put in place. It was then up to the transported inhabitants to live out their lives the best way possible.

On the Moon.

EVERY PICTURE TELLS A STORY

There's that saying every picture tells a story, maybe this isn't true of the one I'm holding in my hand. It shows a family of four; mum, dad, teenage son and daughter, smiling for the camera on a sunny afternoon at the village summer fair.

To be honest they had settled in the small community quite quickly. Mum and dad always there to lend a hand when it was needed, especially for the old folk. The son and daughter were always well mannered and liked by their teachers at school, but maybe not so much by their peer groups. A bit weird or creepy some of them would say. If the other parents were aware of their children's reluctance to befriend the brother and sister they never said anything. It was a small village community and everyone tried to get along as much as possible. Of course it helped that the family were the wealthiest in the borough and had donated a lot of money to various projects, to enhance and improve the village.

There were some conversations though that maybe were a little troubling, it turns out the children were being fostered. Nothing wrong with that, it was the circumstances of how this had come about. I say fostered because both of their parents were still alive, although it turns out, only just. Also this wasn't their first foster home, there had been issues apparently with previous foster parents. To those in the know, the children wouldn't settle because they felt the previous homes provided for them, were below their expectations. These children had come from a fairly wealthy background and wouldn't settle for any less than they were used to.

Consequently the brother and sister had made life very difficult for the previous foster families. However, when they were placed with their present family, who needless to say fitted the financial criteria the two teenagers were willing to accept, all had appeared to be going well. At last social services could breathe a sigh of relief.

People in the village were naturally curious about the children, fuelled by the fact they kept themselves apart from the others in their age group. Initially when they had first moved to the village the other kids had made attempts to befriend them, but the offers of inclusion had been rejected.

Some put it down to the tragic circumstances of their parents accident. Although it had to be said, no one was quite sure what the actual truth was. Different rumours had spread around the village when the family arrived and moved into the big house. However, it was one of the boys from school who was always on the internet had told his parents he had found news reports concerning the accident. It was true there were no photographs of the brother and sister, obviously because of their ages to protect their identities. There was though a photo of the mum and dad which had been taken before they suffered their horrific injuries. The family likeness the boy had argued was too much of a coincidence.

It turns out there had been a burglary at the family home. The mum and dad had been savagely beaten, it was a miracle they were still alive. Apparently an unexpected visit from a neighbour seems to have panicked the attackers and they appeared to have fled the scene, though forensics never found much evidence of them being there. The two children were found huddled in the locked bathroom. Their parents were never able to give any statements as a result of their injuries, as they had suffered catastrophic brain damage. They were both now cared for in a specialist nursing home.

All their assets and wealth were now being managed by financial advisors and everything was held in trust for the children until the death of both parents. So it wasn't a complete surprise but still a shock for the boy who had discovered their identities, when early one morning a fleet of police cars, sirens wailing passed through the village on their way to the big house. Both brother and sister were arrested and charged with the attempted murder of their parents.

It was reported they showed no emotion either at the time of their arrest or at any time throughout the trial, despite the harrowing evidence given in court. This was all the result of dogged determination of a detective on the case, who had spent hours and hours looking at the forensics, despite his superiors reprimanding him for wasting his time on a gut instinct. He had proved the children, incomprehensible as it may seem that two young teenagers from a good loving home could commit such heinous acts. The motive was purely money and the need for materialistic items the two defendants thought they were naturally entitled to, but denied by their parents. Who truly believed they were bringing their children up with a sense of the value of things.

THE UNEXPECTED RETURN

Jean looked at her watch to check the time. She was meeting a friend for lunch and was running a bit late. Just as she put her coat on the doorbell rang. Who can that be she thought, I'm not expecting anyone. Jean was certainly not expecting the man who stood on the doorstep, as she opened the door.

'My god.' She said as she let out a gasp. 'You should be dead!'

Graham her husband brusquely pushed passed her into the hallway.

'Well yes I would have been if your plans had worked out, but here I am my sweet, and you look delighted to see me.' He said in that sarcastic voice she so hated.

'You haven't changed a bit my darling, in what nearly seven years? You almost thought you had made it, didn't you Jean? Then you could officially get my death certificate, and all you survey would finally become yours.'

He winked at her as he said this.

If Jean had had a knife in her hand at that point she would have plunged it through his heart, there and then without a second thought to the consequences.

'I could have made it back home a year ago, but apart from the fact I was enjoying my life; I wanted you to be on the countdown to your freedom. Then I could snatch it away at the eleventh hour.'

'Where have you been all these years?' Jean responded.

She felt as if all the air had been sucked from her lungs, and any minute she may collapse to the ground.

‘In South Africa darling, where you left me. Remember on the trip of a lifetime, for me anyway. Fulfilling my lifelong ambition to see a Great White Shark. I eventually got hold of the news headlines at the time of my disappearance. The photo of you, the distraught wife in tears. The report stated that my body had yet to be found, the boat crew on the hired boat, claimed I had stumbled on the edge of the deck while trying to take photos. I fell overboard and the crew were unable to save me as the Great White carried me off into the ocean.’

‘What you didn’t know my sweet was, the captain of the boat was greedy. He took your money to arrange my tragic demise, and then he told me of your plan. The captain told me he may be a crook and partial to a bit of piracy, but murder was not his game.’

‘So why did you wait all this time, you bastard?’ She spat out the words with all the venom she felt for him.

‘Oh well, there is the rub my dear. I did have an accident on the boat, quite a nasty one actually. While i was attempting to take a spectacular photo of the shark we had spotted, in my excitement I wasn’t really paying attention to my surroundings. The next thing I had tripped and hit my head hard on the side of the boat. Can you believe that? I suffered a fractured skull and bleeding on the brain. It was touch and go for quite a few weeks apparently. The captain and crew of the boat not wanting to appear complicit in your plans, and knowing I had nothing on me to identify who I was. You had kept everything back at the hotel. I was ceremoniously dumped at the local hospital. Surmising I probably wouldn’t survive anyway, in any case they would deny any knowledge of my accident. I could have suffered a fractured skull anywhere.”

‘Ok, enough of all that.’ Said Jean impatiently. I will say again why wait all this time?’

‘Well for weeks I was in an induced coma and when I was finally brought out of it, I had no memory of who I was, or where I was from. I had quite a good life over there, people were very kind. I worked in kitchens and bars, and earned enough for a roof over my head. Then about eight months ago, a couple of tourists walked into a bar I was working in. It turns out they knew me vaguely from a house I had sold them years ago. They were now living in South Africa, I wasn’t sure about them at the time. But slowly and surely over the next few months my memory returned. I didn’t see the couple again, I think they got the impression I was running away from something. But now here I am safe and sound, to rescue our miserable lives together. Now what can you offer me for lunch, my sweet. I’m ravished.”

STALKING

They sit side by side, comrades in arms. Never diverting their focus from the task in hand. They weren't new to this, no they had a lot of experience over many years. Nevertheless each time was given as much attention and dedication as every time before. The tension in the air was palpable. From their crouching down position they had a clear view of their intended target. The element of surprise was definitely theirs. Then the target appeared from over the fence. Springing into action, the three little canines hurled themselves across the garden, barking frantically all the way.

THE PALS

She pushed open the living room door, tray of food in hands.

'Here you are darlin, your favourite Shepherds Pie.'

The old man didn't respond. Motionless, staring at the framed photo in his hands. A half dozen of his closest pals from the war, he had taken the photo all those years ago. They had all died together that day 6th June 1944.

Stan badly wounded had never married, a solitary man.

'I'm ready.' He whispered.

As he took his last breath, she dropped the tray to the floor. The photo changed to show seven smiling young men.

GIRLS NIGHT OUT

Walking back to her car on the multi storey car park, she smiled to herself. It had been a good night, the rock concert was the best she had ever been too. Finally getting to see her favourite band. It had been even more special because she also got to spend the evening with her friend Amy, who she hadn't seen in ages.

The car park was almost deserted now. She and Amy had decided to go to a bar after the concert, before Amy had to get her train home. It was a good catchup and a promise not to leave it so long next time.

She had come out of the lift on the sixth floor and started walking towards the ramp, up to the next floor where her car was parked. Then she heard the scream. Turning in the direction it came from, she saw a hooded figure raising its arm in a stabbing action holding the victim from behind. Driving a weapon into the chest and abdomen. Transfixed she must have let out a cry, because the assailant releasing their grasp on the victim, looked over in her direction.

Cowardly or not? She would reflect later, she turned around and bolted for the lift. Her heart was beating so hard she thought it might explode in her chest. Once inside the lift she frantically pushed the ground button. She couldn't bear to look through the closing doors in case the man, she was sure it was a man; would reach the doors and prevent them from closing.

She reached the ground floor praying there would be passers by on the main street. There was a group of people, possibly students across the road. She couldn't cross as there were too many taxis up and down the thoroughfare. She shouted help to the group across the road, but they ignored her. She tried to flag down a taxi, but even one that was lit for hire drove straight past.

I can't stay here she thought and started to run towards the tram station. There were no plans for her to stay at her boyfriends tonight, and he may be asleep by now, nevertheless she needed him. So she jumped on the tram that would take her to his city centre apartment. She hadn't purchased a ticket, but under the circumstances that was the least of her concerns.

She looked around nervously expecting to see the hooded figure. There were only a few passengers and none of them appeared remotely interested in her. Sitting down heavily on the nearest seat, trying to stop the bile rising up in her throat. Then it occurred to her, she should have phoned the police or an ambulance. The person may still be alive, though judging by the savagery of the attack she thought this was highly unlikely. Risking that she may be in trouble, but hoping the police would understand her flight from the scene, she decided she would just get to Nick's apartment and phone from there.

Desperately ringing on the buzzer to Nick's, there was no answer. Looking at her watch it was now 1.25am. She knew he had an important meeting to attend at 8.30 that morning and he would be in bed now. Surely the buzzer would wake him, she even shouted down the intercom, for him to let her in. Ridiculous she knew but she really needed to be safe in his arms. I know, she thought, I'll phone him. After three attempts she gave up, his phone must be on silent.

The only thing she could do now was to get to the police station, at least there she would be safe. After a nervous twenty minute half run half walk, she arrived at the city station. On entering the building the place was in uproar. Apparently there had been two teenage gangs making war on each other, and one or two of the gang members had been shot, one fatally!

There was a lot of shouting and pushing between the youths who had been cautioned and arrested. The police officers were trying to keep the two gangs separate while they got them down to the cells.

This is crazy, she thought, I'm trying to do the right thing here and report what is probably a murder, and I can't even get to speak with someone. Resigned to the situation for the time being, while the chaos continued, she spotted a chair in a corner of the room. Sitting down, should she phone for an ambulance? Yes she could do that much at least. Phoning 999 requesting an ambulance, there must be something wrong with the signal on her phone. The operator kept asking 'which service she needed?' An ambulance she repeated at least ten times, before she gave up.

Then she noticed it had all gone very quiet and order had been restored, with those arrested now safely locked up for the night. Feeling exhausted she stood up and headed for the duty sargent at the desk. Was that her name mentioned just then, she turned around to the entrance and there was Nick with a police officer. Nick was crying, she reached out to touch him as she said his name. It was as if she wasn't there. He kept his head down and showed no acknowledgment of her presence.

She stood and watched as he was led to the desk and gave his name. Then she noticed his hands were cuffed behind his back. There was blood on his hands. Her blood? Then she felt the agonising pain in her body where he had forced the knife into her.

Then she feels the cold hard ground of the car park, lying there while her life seeps away.

GIRLS NIGHT OUT (HIS STORY)

He had just come in from work, his head was pounding. Throwing his keys on the kitchen counter top, he walked into the bathroom. Opening the cabinet he reached for the paracetamol. He was trying to keep calm.

Don't overthink things, he told himself. She loves you, she has told you many times. You can trust me, she had said. I won't treat you the way she did, I would never do that. She reiterated as she pulled him towards her, putting her arms around his waist and hugging him tightly. He had kissed her forehead.

'I know,' he said 'I know.'

Come and live with me? He had asked her more than once. We have been together a while now.

'Six months.' She had said in her gentle voice. 'Lets see how we are in another six months. Also you know I can't leave my dad at the moment, he's still not coping with mum walking out on him. He's never been good on his own.'

Sitting at his kitchen counter with his microwave meal, his hands gripping the knife and fork so hard his knuckles were turning white. Why is it? He thought women can be so hurtful and destructive. He truly believed he loved Vicky with all his heart, but could he trust her? He had loved and trusted Karen, until he found her in bed with that bastard she worked with. The one she claimed she couldn't stand. He had been suspicious about the two of them for months. That particular day, Karen had said she wasn't going into work, her migraine was too bad. She had even asked him to phone work for her, as she didn't want to lose a days pay.

Was Vicky really on a girls night out with her friend Amy? She had never mentioned any Amy in the six months they had been together. Who was she really going to the concert with? He had offered to go with her, even though it was not his kind of music. No, she had said. Don't be silly you won't enjoy a minute of it. Of course what she actually meant was, she wouldn't enjoy it with me there. I can see right through you Karen, he thought. I mean Vicky, he corrected himself. He picked up his meal and threw it at the wall. Why is she doing this to me? I need to be calm and rational for my assessment in the morning. I told Vicky it was a business meeting, at 8.30am sharp. That's when she said. I won't come back to yours then, it will be late and I don't want to disturb you. How very convenient he had thought, that would give her the opportunity to stay the night with someone else. If he found out who it was, he would kill him.

Looking at his phone it was just coming up to 9pm. He couldn't stay in his apartment, he had to know who she was with. He phoned a taxi to pick him up and take him to the venue where she said she was going. He knew she was driving, so he would get to the car park in plenty of time to find her car. There he would wait and confront her with what he now believed was the truth. Hell! He might even catch them together. He started on the ground floor, checking every vehicle until he found her's. Christ, he muttered to himself. He was running out of time. Quite a few people had already left the concert, presumably to beat the queue getting off the car park. By now he was up on the sixth floor; then the thought occurred to him, she may not even be at the concert. But then wait a minute she had come round to his apartment a few days ago, proudly showing off her ticket she had paid an arm and a leg for. Then looking up the next ramp he saw the car registration plate he recognised.

His feet were going numb from standing on the cold concrete floor. Where was she? It was nearly one in the morning, her car was the only one left on this floor. He had been stood here for nearly three hours now and had got some very strange looks from the people returning to their cars.

‘Waiting for the girlfriend.’ He had said casually to a few people who he thought were paying too much attention to him.

Wait, he could hear footsteps approaching, he would know her footsteps anywhere. He went to conceal himself behind a thick concrete pillar. Hah. He thought, he couldn’t be that good; she wasn’t staying the night with him, whoever he was. They must have had a quicky somewhere. That thought made him feel worse. How could she betray him like that? He felt the cold metal of the carving knife protruding from his jacket sleeve. There she was, her back to him unlocking her car. Stepping towards her quickly and silently, grabbing her from behind one arm across her throat. He plunged the knife into her body. She screamed just the once, though he kept on stabbing her until he let go and she crumpled to the ground. He turned, he thought for a minute someone was there and had seen what he had done; the car park was empty.

The bitch, how could she do this to him. He had to get home now, aware he only had a few hours before the meeting with the Mental Health Team. Damn, he thought he had been doing so well.

COLD BLOODED AMBITION

I would have got it eventually. That much he was sure of. He had always been the best candidate for the post. Anyone with any kind of intelligence could see that. Despite his confidence, the committee hadn't seen it as clearly as he did. More fool them, it was just as well he had taken matters into his own hands. He had saved them the embarrassment of what a mistake they had made. Driving his car at his rival, who was cycling to the meeting. Bloody eco warrior, he thought as he heard bones and metal being crushed

THE VICAR'S PLIGHT

'That's a polite way of saying it's all in her mind. Don't you believe anything she has told us?'

'No, I most certainly don't!' Said the vicar 'I think she's completely insane.'

'That's a bit harsh.' Replied the verger.

'Well that's the conclusion, I've come to, do you have a better explanation?'

'I suppose not,' said the verger 'although she seemed very sincere with her warning for you.'

'It's all ridiculous!' Said the cantankerous vicar.

With that he walked out of the church, as the weathervane fell from the church roof and impaled him to the ground.

THE GRANDE

'Come on,' said Ben. 'You're going to love it up on the mountain side looking down on the fabulous views.'

'I really don't think so.' Said Cathy. 'It's much more your kind of thing, I'm quite happy to have a nice lunch and catch up with Susan, while you do your challenge or whatever you think it is.'

Cathy was trying very hard to keep any kind of sarcasm out of her voice. Her and Ben hadn't been getting on too well over the last few months. There seemed to be more differences between them than there ever used to be. She knew the honeymoon period only lasted so long but she had put her hopes into this relationship. She wasn't getting any younger and she wanted to feel settled. That was one of the reasons she had changed her will last year. Estranged from her grown up children, they had always favoured their father, she had left them a token amount but the bulk of her estate was to be left to Ben.

Of course Ben had protested this was unnecessary, he had a fairly decent job as a reporter on the local rag. This was how they had met, when he came to do a story about Cathy buying the only hotel in the small country village. She was completely renovating it, Cathy had a good business head and had seen the potential. She hadn't been wrong, the village was an up and coming place with cafe bars and deli food outlets, attracting the young professionals from the nearby city who wanted to experience the countryside in small doses.

The hotel also had a bar open to non residents and this had proved popular especially with the younger residents of the village. The older residents preferring to give their business to the local pub, as they had always done. Ben worked his day job covering stories about sheep straying on the main roads. The latest events to be held at the local community centre, and lately, unwelcome travellers stealing expensive garden ornaments from the local's gardens. Ben proved very popular with the younger female clientele, and Cathy being several years older than Ben, found his sometimes outrageous flirting more than annoying. When she had told him to tone it down a bit, he just said she was being overly sensitive, she was the only woman for him. Just lately though he had seemed distant and distracted, putting his phone away quickly if she walked into the room. She loved this man but she would not be made a fool of, so she taken the steps of hiring a private detective. In fact she was waiting for a phone call from him this very morning. If she did give in and do this walk with Ben, which meant so much to him apparently, she needed to know he had been faithful to her.

'So are we doing this?' Said Ben.

'Yes if it will make you happy, but you have to go at my pace. I haven't done anything like this for years.'

'I will take care of you.' He replied 'It will be great and you can't live in the shadow of The Grande without ever having experienced it.'

'Yes I can, I've done very well up until now.' Said Cathy with a wry smile on her face. At that moment her mobile phone rang, Cathy picked it up recognising the number.

'Yes thank you.' She said. 'I understand what you're saying, thank you for getting back to me, I'll be in touch. Goodbye.'

'Who was that?' Ben asked curiously while keeping a smile on his face.

Did he suspect thought Cathy.

'That was Cliff from the linen company, he wants to show me their new range of bedding. He has some good deals at the moment.'

'Oh okay, shall we get ourselves sorted. I've arranged with Beth she will be on reception until we get back, is that alright with you?'

'Of course, just give me half an hour. You can be sorting out the rucksack while your waiting. Make sure you put some energy bars in there.'

'All done.' Ben replied. 'I'll get my gear on as well. I love you darling, thanks for doing this, it means more to me than you will ever know.'

*****

They had only been walking up the steep slope for about an hour on the ascent up The Grande, when it started to rain. Only light at first but some of the clouds coming over the valley looked quite ominous.

'Did you check the weather report Ben?'

'I did yes, this rain wasn't forecast until later this evening,'

'Well if it gets any worse I'm turning back.' Complained Cathy.

'Just give t a bit longer, there are some fantastic views a bit further along.'

After another forty minutes of walking, Cathy was getting tired and very wet. I don't know why I agreed to this, what is the matter with me? She thought. She did know why, she had felt guilty about the phone call this morning, apparently there was nothing to report. The private investigator had found nothing to suggest Ben was up to anything with anyone. Maybe she needed to put more into the relationship. That was why she was here now up this steep hillside, soaking wet.

Ben had dropped behind a little on the narrow path. He said he would let Cathy set the pace, but to be a bit careful some parts of the pathway had quite a steep drop. As Cathy really didn't like heights she was avoiding the temptation to look down. Concentrating on focusing her eyes on the ground ahead, still wishing she hadn't agreed to this.

Ben watched her carefully making her way. The anger inside him welling up. How dare she check up on him. Luckily him and Jimmy, professionally known as James Whitaker PI, had known each other a good few years and Jimmy owed Ben. A few years previously, the two men had been on a drunken night out. There had been a hit and run with Jimmy being the driver, killing a woman who had been on a crossing. They had dumped the car and set it alight, then claiming they discovered the car had been stolen from outside Ben's flat, when they returned from their night out. With no witnesses and no evidence to suggest otherwise, the matter had gone away. Much to the anguish of the woman's family who wanted answers.

So when Jimmy realised who the man Cathy Pearson wanted investigating, he felt more than obliged to contact Ben. This way he would pay off his debt to Ben and still make some money from his fees to Cathy. What could be the harm in that. Admittedly not very scrupulous, but needs must.

They were approaching the part of the walk that Ben had been psyching himself up for. He could do this, he told himself. Just one little nudge. A fall at that point would almost certainly prove fatal, and of course to an inexperienced walker like Cathy, would be put down to a tragic accident. Even the weather had fallen in his favour to substantiate his story.

This was it, he reached forward to grab her coat and throw her down the ravine.

'Hey, be careful there.' Came a male voice from behind him.

As he and Cathy turned round to see who had given the warning, Ben lost his balance on a moss covered stone. Cathy tried to reach out to stop him falling backwards, but her feet wouldn't move. Her fear of heights rooting her to the spot, in doing so saving her life. Not so Ben as his screams echoed around the ravine as he fell to his almost certain death.

The report of the tragic accident was in the local paper. Experienced walkers shook their heads in dismay, they would not have attempted that particular walk in those wet conditions. The park ranger who had witnessed the accident and had shouted the warning to the couple, had been looking for a stray dog. Reportedly belonging to the travellers, it had been seen chasing sheep on the hillside.

The female editor of the local paper sobbed silent tears of regret as she typed out the obituary dedicated to her beloved Ben.

PERPETUATION

I guess life could have been very different. Could it have been better, or who knows, worse? Fate takes you by the hand and leads you down it's winding path. You can never be sure what's coming next, despite all your planning and expectations, hopes and ambitions. There are surprises and disappointments, all have to be dealt with, happy or sad. Seasons turn into years, decades go by. Governments in power change, but life goes on the same. Nature perpetuates itself year on year, thank god, despite what we do. Lives loved and lost, and so it goes on.

DREAMS

She awoke in a cold sweat and looked around her familiar bedroom, everything was as it should be. The dream had come again, the one where she murders someone. She never actually sees her victim, that isn't the worst part of the dream. It's all about her fear of being found out. So when she wakes, it is with a flood of relief, it was just a dream. But not this time. She gets out of bed and reaches for her dressing gown, her hands are smeared with blood. She knows with absolute dread the dream has become a reality.

GOLDDIGGER

'Good morning Mrs O'Dowd.'

'Morning.' She replied grudgingly to the postman.

'Shall I put these in your letterbox as you're on your way out?'

'Yes.' She said without a please or a thank you, as she turned to get in her car.

The postman pushed the letters through the letterbox and whispered, miserable bitch, under his breath.

She had to go to the village to pick up some groceries. She would buy her husband's favourite piece of steak from the butchers, even though he wouldn't be eating it. That thought brought a secret smile to her not unattractive face. The problem with this small village was everybody knew your business. She hated it. It was his idea good old Ernie, to move here when he retired and everybody liked him. She knew what they said behind her back. *How come a lovely man like that could be married to such a witch.*

She didn't care, she had married Ernie a few years ago after his first wife died. After nursing both her parents until their untimely deaths, there was a need for a new life and some financial security. They, her parents had left her nothing, all their wealth had been poured down their throats. The way she saw it, she was owed a life and Ernie with his nice fat pension scheme and no kids to provide for, was manna from heaven.

Their courtship had been a difficult time for her. She wasn't used to being nice for such long periods of time. Luckily Ernie wasn't that keen on the sexual side of things. Perhaps because he was still grieving for his dearly departed wife. Their relationship certainly hadn't gone down well with his family, especially his sister Mary.

Golddigger, she had heard her saying on their wedding day. Cheeky cow, she had thought, but she had to admit dear Mary was right.

Everything was going reasonably well after they married. She didn't mind living in the big detached house he had shared with his wife. In fact she loved it and she even let Ernie keep some of his wife's belongings, so he could go and have a cry over them, now and again. Pathetic was the word that came to mind, but each to his own. Anyway, there was nothing better than a bit of retail therapy though Ernie never saw the attraction. He did complain once that she could never possibly wear all the clothes and shoes she bought. So then she switched to expensive jewellery, always a good investment. Being twenty two years younger than her husband, she didn't want to be impoverished in her old age.

Damn him though when he decided they were to move to the country. She tried everything to dissuade him, anger, tears, threats to leave him, which of course she had no intention of doing. Even the promise of sex, which she now found she quite liked with the odd job man come gardener, he employed. Ernie's weekly visits to his sister's house were a source of delight to her. He wouldn't change his mind though, she had never seen him so adamant. Perhaps he did want her to leave, well that wasn't going to happen. She had invested a lot of precious time and energy into their marriage.

This god damn village though, how she hated it, full of banal people with small mentalities. She hadn't meant to kill him, not yet at least, but he had annoyed her so much. When she broached the subject of her having a little holiday by herself; she was missing the odd job man, Rob. It had been two months since their move to the village and distance certainly made the heart grow fonder, well actually it was just lust. When she finally got her hands on Ernie's estate, she wasn't going to share it. To her amazement her husband just said no! They couldn't afford it, her spending has seriously depleted his pension.

Well that was it, she had picked up the heavy 17th century candlestick from the fireplace and whacked him on the back of his head as he turned his back on her. Their conversation apparently done with. She had wrapped his lifeless body in the rug from the hallway and dragged him out to the woodshed. It had been there for a few days now, good job it was the middle of winter and the nights had been sub zero, with the days not much warmer.

She needed time to think things through, hence the facade of buying his favourite cut of steak. During the visit to the butchers previously, she had the foresight to mention to the busybody butcher, that Ernie was a bit under the weather at the moment. Keep all options open was her plan, but still the big hole in his head and his decaying body were going to take some explaining. However, she was nothing if not resourceful. Her parents of course had been so much easier. Burned to death in their own beds, from a dropped cigarette butt. While she was having a much deserved weekend break in London. She was slightly put out she never actually got to the West End musical she had a ticket for. You but can't be in two places at once.

What had really complicated the situation now, was when his interfering sister turned up at the cottage because she hadn't heard from him in a few days. Mary being her usual annoying self wouldn't accept the explanation that he had laryngitis and was safely tucked up in bed asleep and he would contact her when he was feeling better.

Mary simply wasn't having it, she pushed her way in and started up the stairs. Bloody cheek. So there was nothing for it but to grab her and throw her down the stairs. Then she hit her head on the marble top of the hall table. Unfortunately, to put her out of her misery she had to be finished off with a cushion. Then unbelievably having wrapped her in a sheet, with the intention of emptying the chest freezer, the doorbell rings. Standing on the doorstep is Mary's bloody husband Stan.

Just how much can one woman take!

THE ADMISSION

Strictly speaking, you might say it was my fault. But did I tell the bus driver to drive under the low bridge? No I did not. I may have removed the *low bridge* sign. Just to see what would happen. After all, we all have free will, don't we? I was exerting mine when I moved the diversion sign so the traffic had to go under the low bridge. So now there's a queue of traffic on both sides. Oh and here comes the emergency vehicles, fire ambulance and police.

It's all in a day's work for them.

THE CHRISTMAS JUMPER

The police car pulled up behind the vehicle parked illegally on the bridge.

'I'll run a check on the reg number.' Said Scott, the male officer. 'Says here it belongs to a Carol Ann Banks.

The two officers got out and walked over to the car, looking inside they could see a handbag on the driver's seat. The car was locked.

'This must be the jumper's car.' Said Carolyn.

'It certainly looks that way.' Replied Scott, as he walked round the back of the car to try the boot.

They both turned to look over the bridge that crossed the motorway. The flashing lights from the emergency vehicles below, reflecting onto their faces. The body of the woman had been hit by at least two vehicles, unable to avoid her as her body had fallen from the bridge onto the carriageway. Though extremely distressing for the motorists involved she most likely died as she hit the ground.

'Some family is going to get some seriously bad news on Christmas Day, of all days. It's probably going to be on us to deliver the news. Are you thinking the same Scott?' Asked Carolyn.

'Yeah more than likely, I hate these jobs, not that I've done many. I would much rather be picking up drunks off the streets, even when they're covered in their own vomit and piss. I'd really like to retrieve the handbag before we radio control for a recovery vehicle. It's possible there's a suicide note in it or anywhere in the car.'

‘These should help.’ Said Carolyn. She had spotted a set of keys on the ground that they hadn’t initially seen when they arrived on scene. Carolyn pressed the key fob, it was one of those keyless entries. The car unlocked she reached in for the bag.

‘There’s a purse and a photo driving license. This definitely belongs to our jumper. It gives her date of birth as 31st October, 1986. That makes her thirty two years old. Here’s her mobile as well, it got several missed calls from a Jamie.’

Once the car had been collected by the recovery vehicle, Scott and Carolyn had been instructed as they thought they would be, to go the address they had and inform any family. They had returned the handbag to the seat of the car for forensics to runs checks on it, together with the car. It appeared the woman had driven to the bridge on her own, but that would need to be established and that it was indeed a suicide. With a lack of witnesses on the bridge and no note found, hopefully they would be able to find out more from any family or friends as to the state of mind of Carol Ann Banks.

Arriving at the address, it was a new build, a neat detached property. There was a car parked on the drive, an Audi Q5. There were lights on in the house, upstairs and down.

‘Looks like someone is at home.’ Said Scott. ‘Are you ready for this partner?’ He gave Carolyn the nod as they got out of the police car.

‘Yep let’s get this over with.’ Carolyn responded. As they approached the front door they could see it was slightly ajar.

‘Hello police.’ Called Carolyn, as she pushed the door fully open. ‘Can we come in?’

There was no reply, but they could hear music coming from one of the rooms off the hallway. It was Slade's Christmas song. *Merry Christmas Everybody.* The two officers looked at each other, both raising their eyebrows, this wasn't going to be easy, but they both understood it never could be.

'Police, can we come through?' Scott called out.

Whatever the officers were mentally preparing themselves for, it certainly wasn't the scene that appeared before them. As they entered the dining room, the music was playing from the Alexa on the side cabinet. There were five adults, three men and two women slumped around a dining room table. Chances are they would have fell off their chairs but for the fact the chair arms were supporting them. They were all motionless. The younger male adult looked to be in his thirties, while the others were probably sixties or seventies. Possibly parents and in-laws. On the table were the remnants of a Christmas dinner. There were two more places set at the table, both with unfinished food on them, the scene was almost macabre. The occupants of the room were all still wearing the colourful paper hats from the Christmas crackers. Possibly the only thing missing was party blowers in their mouths, where instead was white foam escaping from their lips.

It was then the two officers heard footsteps behind them. As they turned a young boy of about ten or eleven years old appeared at the door.

'Have you found my mum?' He said. 'I think they are all dead.' He pointed to the people at the table. 'I've been calling her but she's not answering her phone.'

'Are you Jamie?' Carolyn enquired in a gentle voice.

‘Yes.’ the boy said. He seemed in a state of shock, not at all surprising considering the circumstances.

‘Can you tell us what happened here Jamie?’ Asked Scott.

‘We were all eating dinner, mum was in one of her weird moods she gets in. I was supposed to be going to my dad’s for Christmas Day, but my step dad wouldn’t let me. He said we all had to be together here with the oldies. My step dad always gets his own way. Mum wasn’t eating much of her food, she said she wasn’t hungry. Then she just got up and went out of the house. My step dad sat for a few minutes looking at us, he had an angry look on his face. Then he went to look for mum but she had already driven off in her car. He came back and said she’ll be back in a bit and we should finish our dinner. I didn’t eat my sprouts, because I hate them, mum knows that. Then I went to my bedroom to phone mum.’

A DAY IN THE LIFE

I've had a good day today. Breakfast at seven, the usual, not bad, I could have eaten more but that's all she gives me. *'That's enough you're on a diet.'* She says. Oh well she must be obeyed, apparently I am getting a little wide around the middle. I still love her anyway. We have been together six and a half years now and she still tells me I'm irresistible.

It's a very pleasant day, dry and warm but not hot. I'm not keen on hot weather. She likes the heat, lay on her sun lounger in the midday sun, I prefer the shade.

In the late afternoon we go out for a nice walk together, nothing much said really. Well there's no need, we are comfortable in our silence, breathing in the fresh air. Occasionally I look at her adoringly and she gives me an indulgent smile.

When we get back home she has things to do, while I potter around the house like I usually do. She doesn't mind, we both know the roles we fulfil.

The grandchildren call round with their mum and she gives them some chocolate. Lucky beggars, I'm not allowed! They smear a lot of it on the kitchen cupboards with their chocolatey fingers. I give her a sideways look, she will have a cloth on that as soon as they have gone. She likes a tidy house which can cause some friction between the two of us. I can be quite messy, however, she knew that when we met and anyway it keeps her busy.

Later on after our evening meal, we don't always eat the same things; we settle down to watch some television. I invariably get bored and decide to get my favourite toy from my basket and drop it in her lap. Whilst wagging my tail expectantly.

(DEDICATED IN MEMORY OF BUSTER)

Printed in Great Britain
by Amazon

32995164R00054